Chand

Zarurat Ishq Ki

Flairs and Glairs

Publication House

"ChandZarurat Ishq Ki"

ISBN No: " 978-93-90416-60-8"
1st Edition
Language – English and Hindi

Flairs and Glairs
Publication House
Regd. Under MSME Act.

Disclaimer

This is a work of fiction and solely represent the thoughts of the corresponding authors of the articles. Our editors have tried their best to edit the content of all the authors and check the plagiarism.

All the write-ups in this book are unique and are only published in this book.

In case any plagiarism or error is found, only the author is responsible alone, and not the publisher or the Compilers.

Cover Designing
Shubham Shah

Acknowledgement

Dear Almighty, thank you for blessing me with the power and zeal to be able to complete this Anthology. Also, Thank You dear parents, for trusting in me, and letting me work whenever I wanted. My family is the one who supported me for what I am today.
When it comes to this Anthology, I would like to start with Thanking the Co-authors, without your help and support, I would have never been able to complete it.

Thank You all of you, for being there. Much Love to all of You. I am glad to see you all standing by me.

Co Authors

1. Shubham Shah (Founder F&G)
2. Shivangi Jaiswal (Compiler)
3. Mina Jaiswal
4. Ishani Agarwal
5. Ishika Agarwal
6. Jyoti Singh Rajput
7. Akash Goswami
8. Isshu Sami
9. Muskan Shah
10. Rubal Choudhary
11. Adamya Tripathi
12. Priyanka Arora
13. Bharat Batra
14. Deepjyoti Chowdhury
15. Mehere Darakshan
16. Hridyansh Bhardwaj
17. Shreya Giri
18. Bushra Shaikh
19. Jata V
20. Jaya Bhardwaj
21. Shaily Tyagi
22. Tayyaba Tabassum
23. Abhilash Rout
24. S. Aarthi
25. Meer Aarifa
26. Abhishek Rawat
27. Disita Sikdar

28.Najudah Tabassum
29.Sachin Banoudhiya
30.Sumit Sharma
31.Swetha D
32.Sourav Bhatia
33.Reena Karamdev Yadav
34.Poorvi Verma
35.Debanjana Ghatak
36.Kartik kumar
37.Sangram Santosh Salgar
38.Bickey Mandal
39.Dr. Harini Chowdary Vadlamudi
40.Shivansh sharma
41.Paulami Kotal
42.Chahat Batra
43.Yash Ojha
44.Saloni Lal Srivastava
45.Grishma Ninave
46.Arju Tiwari
47.Abhiraj Gautam
48.S Prakash
49.Megha Arora
50.Karan singh
51.Ishani Durba Purkayastha
52.Payal Singhal
53.Pratiksha Ghatge
54.Abha Bindal
55.Vickey David
56.Manali Chowdhury

57.Vikesh Krishna Jalmi Alias Gawde
58.Rakhi Krishnani
59.Anita Zalwal
60.Parul Sunder
61.Tathambika
62.Mausam Agrawal
63.Ovita Ekka
64.Priya Jogadia
65.Vrunda Kumbhar
66.Pragya kapil
67.Mihika Saraf
68.Arijit Mondal
69.Stuti Mahesh Naik
70.Abhilash Sharma
71.Diya Mehta
72.Rani singh
73.Parwana Bibi
74.Isha
75.Abhishek Gupta
76.Meenakshi Sharma
77.Dipti David
78.Chirag L Sagar
79.Ayushi bhatnagar
80.S. Deeksha
81.Disha Dulani
82.Richa Gupta
83.Vaishni Venkatesh
84.Shobhana Serana
85.Aafreen Saleem

86.Sayandeep Patra
87.Krushnapriya Behera
88.Dulgach Pooja Singh
89.Ronak Jain
90.Jayant Jain
91.Reshmi Maheshwar Vernekar
92.Rittwika Sharma
93.Neha Chanda
94.Jovita Ekka
95.Megha P. Yadav
96.Aarushi Singh
97.Vishal Sharma
98. Siya Golani
99.Heena Shaikh Mulla
100.   Nilanjana Sarkar
101. Jaspreet Kaur
102. Astha Yadav
103. Dr. Ruchita Chauhan
104. Sandhya Kanojiya
105. Divyanshi Goel

Shubham Shah

(Founder- Flairs and Glairs)

Shubham Shah, entrepreneur at "Flairs & Glairs" a brand with dynamics in events organizing and cultural educational pan INDIA, He is a 26yr. old guy who recently has entered, the digital platform of imprinting emotions. He has initiated with his own open mic platform to help budding poets and aspiring writers under his brand named as "Teekhe Zasbaaat"

He is a commerce graduate from Bhagalpur City of Bihar.

He says Writing has impersonated him since childhood and he has now been writing for over a decade!

Cooking, on the other hand, is his passion! He also mentions, trying out new things just tickles him!

When asked sir, Why SPICY EMOTIONS?

He smiled and added, "agar jasbaat teekhe na ho toh wo jasbaat kaha" Spices are all that blends! So do his words!
As a chef, he presents to you his dish! Hot and freshly served! Taste it! Feel it! Enjoy it! You can also find his writing in the Solo book "Teekhe Zasbaaat" and 70+ anthologies. With his passion to explore opportunities across Platforms he is working with keen devotion and We wish him all the very best for his future ventures
Share your reviews on his

INSTAGRAM

@spicy_emotions
@shubham4shah

Or via email on

shubham2shah@gmail.com

To stay tuned to his work and opportunities follow his business Handles

INSTAGRAM   FACEBOOK   YOUTUBE

@flairsandglairs
@teekhezasbaaat

WEBSITE:

https://flairsandglairs.in/
https://flairsandglairs.com/

Shivangi Jaiswal

(Compiler)

Shivangi Jaiswal is a Content Writer from Kolkata. Project Head & Coordinator at "Flairs & Glairs" brand with dynamics in events organizing and cultural educational pan INDIA. Organiser at "The Glittering Fables" Writing Community. She is a B.Com Honours graduate. Certified in Stocks & Short Selling as well as Certified in Digital Marketing Been a keen student, she has recently been Certified for learning Spanish Language..She loves to bring smiles and happiness to many faces, so she is into social service. Shivangi has also done her Diploma in painting, drawing and all kinds of clay making, craft works. Traveler, Teacher, Meditator, Dancer, Singer,

Instrument Player. She loves to play guitar and harmonium. Been a public speaker she has taken part in many events and nailed it. Also been a great Advisor to many. Sports freak of Swimming and Badminton with a passion so strong. Since, past one year she has started her writing journey. She writes so that many people can connect with their stories and get positive hopes. She thinks " Every story is unique so embrace yourself to the best".She is a writer by day and a reader by night. Been a Complier of 15+ Anthologies, and in process for more, also Co- authored 60+ anthologies. Shivangi is an old soul with young eyes, a vintage heart, and a beautiful mind."

You can follow her work:

Instagram

@the_knockingvibe

@house_of_compilations

Moon Love

Laying down on the grass,
Looking upon the skies.

The beauty of Moon Light
was just so elegant and bright.

While seeing the moon,
I searched for a sign of
love to be found.

As the stars sparkled in the sky,
While I was thinking of You & I.

Isn't it beautiful? Yes.
The moon with a beauty of
grace glowing upon the sky.

Moon O Moon
You are the witness of true love.

Illuminating my path as I walk down the streets,

You are my way,
You are my Destination...

My better half,
My Love Moon.

Moon Light Story

My love for you will always remain constant.
As the moon spreads it's light all over the world.
With happiness, love, joy all over.

I will be always there shining by your side.
Beauty are in the nights.
Where the moonlight pours love between us.
Listening to your heartbreak
Leaning at your chest.

The love with every beat of your heart.
Makes me closer to you.
A confession night
When he asked me at the moon light?
Marry me?
I smiled and said "Yes".

Finally, a moonlight story was
Glowing bright high in the night skies

.

A Moonlight Love

Laying under the sky,
I see a gentle glow of light.
The Moonlight that glowed
between us.

As we gazed deep into
each other's eyes.
Lying so close to me.
Underneath the sky
Only You & I.

This moonlight sky was witness of our love.
The silvery beams cast soft upon your face.
As arms grapped into each other's embrace.
 The pink lips seem to glow more as the moon light showers
her beauty.

The touch of you,
Together our hearts started beating.
The kiss of us, now couldn't make us apart.
The tender of our touch under the moonlight.
Melody of words composed in love.

Together we made a moonlight love.

(1)

Look how beautiful is the moon
Quiet, Silent, beautiful, smoothing
Full of love just like you.

(2)

Kitna adhoora sa lagta hai
Raat Chand ke bina,
Jab koi apna ho, par paas na ho
Jab zindagi ho, par khwaish na ho
Jab ankhein ho, par khwaab na ho
Or jab shikayat ho, par sune wala koi na ho..
Kitna adhoora sa lagta hai.
Par waqt ke sath badal jana hi sahi rehta hai.

चाँद

शाम होते चाँद का इंतज़ार करती हूँ ॥

और जो बादलों की ओट में छिपी रहती ॥

मैं उसे बातें करती तो वह सामने आती ॥

अपने साथ शीतलता लाती ॥

मैं उस चाँद को प्यार से निहारती ॥

अपने गम, खुशियों की बातें करती ॥

और चाँद सितारों के बीच मैं मुस्कुराती रहती ॥

चाँद दुर दरार से अपनों का संदेश लाता
और सारी खुशियां दे जाता ॥

- Mina Jaiswal

You Are Beautiful.

I look at the moon and wonder

How can something be so far,

Yet be so beautiful and dear..

But then,

I also realize,

You are far.. yet you are so near..

If your coldness still makes you beautiful in my eyes,

Then how can the moon be ugly ?

Ishani Agarwal

When the moon is absent

Just like the night sky, there is absence of love in my heart.

Without the moon, there is no excitement in life.

Without the moon, there is no light in my eyes.

As the moon returns, love and excitement returns.

It reminds me of you, my love.

Without you is just like sky without moon.

I feel empty inside and out without you.

I miss you,

I will love you always.

–Ishika Agarwal

आज अरमानों को बेहेक जाने दो
जज़्बातों की मेहेक फलक तक जाने दो...

आज अरमानों को बेहेक जाने दो

जज्बातों की मेहेक फलक तक जाने दो

हर सांस को एहसासों से सजाने दो

दश्त-ए-जीस्त को आज उल्फत के गीत गाने दो

लम्हा-लम्हा रूमानियत में रम जाने दो

लबों को लबों की नमी चुराने दो

तन्हाइयों को तिश्नगी आज मिटाने दो

कतरा-कतरा हिज्र का गर्म पनाहों में जल जाने दो

शब-ए-वस्ल में खामोशी को मुस्कुराने दो

नूरे चांदनी में आज जश्ने इश्क मनाने दो...

–Jyoti Singh Rajput
(IG: @the_ frozen_flame_2801)

॥ इश्क़ की चाँदनी ॥

रिश्ते-ए-वफ़ा पर अब कोई ज़िद्द नहीं थी,
मेरे चाँद को धूप कभी पसंद नहीं थी,
आईना भी जिससे हया कर जाए,
चाँद नहीं, वो बला का रूप थी।

ना ही मुद्दतों जुदा थे,
कहाँ सुबह-हो-शाम साथ थे,
घर के आँगन से हम दोनों,
बस! लुका-छुपी खेलें सारी रात थे।

एक रोज़ कुछ यूँ हुआ था,
छुप गई थी वो रूठ कर,
मैंने चाँदनी को इश्क़ कहा था,
वो चिढ़ गई थी बस इस बात से।

धीमे-धीमे रातें बीतें,
ये अमावस बीते, लगे जैसे साल
इश्क़ जैसे ही कफ़स लगे
लो! मुद्दतों बाद आ गया चाँद ॥

Akash Goswami

(IG: @manzarakash)

Gila!

Chand na Gaya kahi magar uski Chandni gayi.
Rota Raha mehboob yahi magar wo lauti nhi.
Khun sukh Kar safed hogya
Khilona-e-dil kahi kho Gaya
Ehsaas har waqt ubalte jate hai
Uske bina hum reh Nahi pate hai.
Zinda rehna ummido ki majburi hai
Mar ne se pehle ek mulaqat zaruri hai
Saba chalti rahi ret udti rahi
Saasein rukti kabhi saasein ukhadti rahi
Meri marzi ka kab hua hai khuda
Wo bichad kr mujhse hua hai dhua..
Koi tasbih pado koi Dua to karo
Uske hatho ki mehndi me naam Mera bharo .
Tassavur me sahi wo Mera toh ho
Jaana jhut magar ek baar toh kaho
Mujhko rato me milne ko aaongi tum
Meri nabz Meri hasi banjaongi tum
Jo Chand ke niche thi nazre mili
Us Chand ki ronak le aaongi tum
Main malmal ke badal bununga sada
Main khoti tumhari sunga sada
Main ashko ki nehre, main badal ghanere, main chubti
chubhan, sare zakhm Jo gehre, sabhi Dil me bhar bhar
basaunga main!
Tujhpe sari Duniya lutaunga main..
Mujhe mere Baki wo din tum dilado
Wo Chand ki chandi hasin tum dilado
Wo gesu siyah wo chehra aftabi
Baatein sukhan ki wo baatein kitabi
Mujhe mere Dil ka laahu Lauta do

Ya chahe toh fir Mera janaza uthado
Mar Kar sukoon agar mil bhi Gaya
Ek shikan hogi shiqayat ke tu na Mila
Or wo Chand karenga sada hi Gila!!

~Isshu Sami

(IG: @Isshu_sami)

How Beautiful Is The Moon You See?

Full of Emitting light and showing all it's beauty.

Moon, A symbol of Love Silence, Purity, and Contentment. It always gives us the power to hold situations when not in control.

-Rubal Choudhary

ये चांद

ये चांद,

आज भी मुझसे मिलने आता है,

जब भी आता है,

वही तुम्हारा वाला गाना गुनगुनाता है,

ये चांद,

आज भी मुझसे मिलने आता है,

जो पूछता हूं मैं तेरे बारे में,

तो कहता है,

क्यों पूछते हो उसके बारे में,

वो तुमसे अलग होकर,

आज भी मुस्कुराता है,

ये चांद,

आज भी मुझसे मिलने आता है...

कहता है,

खुश हो तुम अपनी जिंदगी में,

अब तुम्हें कोई गम नहीं है,

पहले जैसे तुम्हारी आँखें,

अब नम नहीं है,

जी रही हो तुम,

अपनी जिंदगी के हसीन लम्हें,

और फिर तेरी तारीफ सुनाता है,

ये चांद,

आज भी मुझसे मिलने आता है...

नसीहतें देता है,

नसीहतें देता है कि भूल जाऊं तुम्हें,

पता है,

उसे कि मेरा आज भी तेरे साथ एक नाता है,

ये पगला चांद,

आज भी मुझसे मिलने आता है,

तुम जैसे भूली हो मुझे,

वैसे ही मुझे तुम्हें भुला देने की,

नसीहतें दे जाता है,

ये पागल चांद,

आज भी मुझसे मिलने आता है...

-Adamya Tripathi

(IG: @adamya_tripathi)

(1)

एक दिन मेरा चाहने वाला

सितारों को मेरे सिर पर सजा

भर देगा मेरी माँग को

ओर बना देगा मुझे चांद सा सुंदर

तब शुरू होगा

प्रेमयुद्ध

आसमान और संसार के

सभी प्रेमी जोड़ों के बीच ।।

~Priyanka ArorA

(IG: Baghlapriyanka)

(1)

Jiski roshni mere dil ko bhaati hai,
Jisko dekhne ke liye sara din aankhein taras jaati hai,
Wo khoobsurat hai bahot aur mera zehnaseeb hai,
Wo koi aur nahi Chaand hai aur mere dil ke kareeb hai,
Dilchasp aisa ke koi nahi jisko dekhne se inkaar ho jaaye,
Manmohak aisa ki dekhte hi isse pyaar ho jaaye,
Chaand aur sitaaron ke siwa koi aur rishta saccha nahi lagta,
Kabhi kabhi ye doobta hua chaand bhi hamko accha nahi lagta,
Man karta hai bas ise ek takk dekhta rahoon,
Kuchh aur na karoon, bas is roshni ko khudme sametta rahoon,
Jab chhup jaata hai badlon me to bahot bura lagta hai,
Isko dekhne ke baad hi din mera poora lagta hai,
Chaand ki roshni ke bina jeena bhi lagta dushwaar hai,
Ho bhi kyu na, aakhir ye Chaand hi to mera pehla pyaar hai

-Bharat Batra

(IG: @bharat_an_independent_poet)

Moon and Sky

Fixed in my life, like the moon in the sky;
The story of our love the universe can testify.
The beautiful conspiracy that got us unified,
Remained constant, though years passed by.

The world tried to separate but we denied,
With tests and tribulations our love was sanctified.
Looking at the moon's loyalty, encouraged to duplify;
With each passing day, the love was multiplied.

Like the moon cannot be separated from the sky,
Though far but we would soon be nearby.
Will love you endlessly until the day I die,
By inking it down, our love I glorify.

-Deepjyoti Chowdhury

(IG: @dj_writes_to_heal)

A Dream Under The Moon

I sleep staring at moon,

Believing he too staring back to me,

He comes down for me and seat besides exactly when my

eyes are closed,

He wake me up and take me with him.

Galaxy are shown ,

Clouds are chased,

Sparkles are gifted,

When every unimportant we talked

Just both of us, universe got surprised.

I feel loved wrapped in faith,

Still can't sense envy from stars.

I Feel loved, rays on my face

That burn me like hell,

Then I wake up in my bed .

My heart is broken,

Scattered as my dream .

My minds speaks to my heart ,

No one is there ,

Just be where you are.

~Mehere Darakshan

(IG: @Coolandcute_suman)

Chand - Mulakat Ke Liye Ek Chandani Rat Jaruri Hai

Kya kahun mein ab mere chand ke baare mein.

Chand mera naraaj hai,

Badlon mein chhupkar baitha hai.

Deedar karna hai mujhe mere chand ka,

Bas andhera hee dikhayi rahaa hai.

Kuch kisse, kuch lamhe aur kuch dard baantne hain mujhe,

Bas nikal bhi aao,

Tumhara hee intzaar ho rahaa hai.

Kya kahun mein ab mere chand ke baare mein.

Tadap aisi hai tumhe dekhne kee,

Ab jeena bhi dushvar lag rahaa hai.

Bas aasmano ko nihar rahaa hoon,

Aur tumhe dekhne kee rab se izazat maang rahaa hoon.

Kya kahun mein ab mere chand ke baare mein.

Aankhe thak chuki hain,

Bas aansu nikle jaa rahe hain,

Iss andhere kee barasat mein,

Ek roshani kee talaash kar rahaa hoon.

Bas ab nikal bhi aao ,

Tumhara hee intzaar kar rahaa hoon.

Kya kahun mein mere chand ke baare mein.

-Hridyansh Bhardwaj

(IG: @hridyansh_bhardwaj)

Rays Of Love

The sun sets to brighten his love,the moon,

With a hope to meet her soon.

But the moon share the night sky with the star,

Who love her despite her scar.

The moon admires the self dependent twinkling one,

And thinks the star to be her source,not the sun.

Every evening, the sun wants to wait,

But cannot deny the universal fate.

The sun keeps the tag of powerful,

And makes the moon look wonderful.

Everyone praises the moon for her beauty,

But, only the setting sun gets the credit of being pretty.

Despite huge explosions on his surface,

He still help the moon to hide her scars of the face.

Unknown to the sun's sacrifice,

The moon thinks star to be wise.

Somehow she cannot accept the star,

As a lover with whom she can go far.

The shooting stars carry desire, wish or prayer.

The moon waits for someone, somewhere.

The couples face the night sky with a hope of togetherness,

The moon dreams of her love , being careless.

She carries messages of love and care,

Crossing the night sky is just a dare,

May be a nightmare.

Will her punishment be spare?

Or she will be lonely!

With a hope only.

But the day arrived soon,

The luckiest day for the moon.

Nobody can see her,

She cried 'where are you star?'.

She cannot see any cloud,

But suddenly saw a big round.

Blue and green in colour,

No! she was not dreaming in summer.

The earth moved away,

She saw her love far away.

She soon faced the shinning rays,

It was the end of countless days.

The lunar eclipse came to an end,

She found her true love and nearest friend.

Now she knew her actual lover,

Her source and care giver.

His warm rays surrounded her surface,

Hugs and kisses all over her body and face.

She reflected back to the sun,

Who got the cold wrapped love ,although he burns.

As love is beyond science ,

Something that rise your conscience.

Love is truth ,trust ,maybe waiting,

Something as sweet as chocolating.

Their dates began to be better,

Sometimes the moon rise faster and sun set later.

They got the chance to say bye,

As they share the same sky.

Just their time is different but world is same ,

They fell in love over and over again.

-Shreya Giri

चांद

तू आये उस चांद के साथ रह जाए मेरी बाहों में मेरे ख्वाब के साथ,

मेरे वक़्त में तू हर वक़्त रह ,

मेरी सांसों में तू हमदम रह,

मेरी रगों में तू हर वक़्त बहे,

तू आये उस चांद के साथ रह जाए मेरी बाहों में मेरे ख्वाब के साथ,

मेरे हर सफर की मंज़िल है तू,

ये याद रहे तुझे हमेशा,

मेरी मुकम्मल जहां का है तू हिस्सा,

तेरे बगैर मेरी हर एक शाम है अधूरी,

मोहब्बत में लाज़िम है ये दूरी,

लेकिन बस यही है मेरी ख्वाहिश की,

तू आये उस चांद के साथ रह जाए मेरी बाहों में मेरे ख्वाब के साथ।

-Bushra Shaikh

(IG: @pyaarlafzoonmain)

Mehtaab And Me

One twilight,
I composed a distinct tune
To my dear best friend
Who asked me to wait in the park...

As soon as she arose,
I became ready with my rose
And with the heart that I had in my tune...
"You and I are...", I started singing.

She just blushed and
Hid behind that pine trees
And jumped behind the clouds!
Deabak! I was super excited...

As the city lights fall asleep,
She put my arms around her.
We danced till dawn silently
In our own little world.

Her shimmering shine lit up
The gloom in my faded life
She's the first whom I fell in love with,
My dearest dear Love, Moon...

-Jata_V

शीर्षक:अब हमारे चांद भी बदल गये हैं क्या?

अब हमारे चांद भी बदल गये हैं क्या?

माना कि माना था जिसे चांद ,

उसकी रोशनी उम्र भर तो ना मिल पायेगी।

हां अमावस तो नहीं होगा,

पर कुछ यादों की धुंध सी छा जायेगी ।

पर, अब हमारे चांद भी बदल गये हैं क्या?

हो सकता है, तुझे उस हुस्न में मेरी झलक भी नजर नहीं आयेगी।

और कुछ रूसवाई, तो कुछ तन्हाई सी कर जायेगी ।

पर, अब हमारे चांद भी बदल गये हैं क्या?

क्या याद है तुम्हें,

मेरे चेहरे को अपना आईना कहा था तुमने ।

फिर क्यों तेरी खुशी तेरा प्रतिबिंब ना बन पाएगी।

तो, अब हमारे चांद भी बदल गये हैं क्या?

-Jaya Bhardwaj
(IG: @ jayakjazbaat)

ए चांद

रुक जा जरा थम जा जरा ए चांद,

नजर मुझे तुझमें मेरा महबूब आता है।

मन की बदलियां भी छठ जाती है,

जब सामने तू नजर आता है ।

तू गवाह है हमारी मोहब्बत की रातों को,

वो कसमो वादों का, वह प्यार भरी बातों का,

रुक जा जरा समझा जरा ए चांद ,

नजर मुझे तुझ में मेरा महबूब आता है ।

खिड़की से देख कर तुझे आज भी सुकून आता है,

ना जाने क्यों तू बीते दिनों की याद दिलाता है।

रुक जा जरा थम जा जरा ए चॉद,

नजर मुझे तुझमें मेरा महबूब आता है।

-Shaily Tyagi
(IG: @Sandhya.tyagi.1232)

O Beloved Moon Look Up

To look at you.
I searched for solace
And found you.
The tears rushed..
Rushed to travel to another world
And they made me to look for you.
O my beloved Moon!
You've always consoled my heart with your nightingale's tune.
Quiet and calm like a morning you were..
Filled with chaos and despair I was..
I always look up,
To look at you.
Whenever the heart aches,
Whenever the mind senses a mistake,
I look up,
To look at you.
O my beloved Moon!
You always listened the me calmly..
And helped me tackle what I was going through.

-Tayyaba Tabassum

(IG: @ The_fictional_lines)

Chandni Raat Ki Vo Baat

Wo bhi kya din the
jahan tum aur hum
milke rehte the,
aur aaj ye din hai
jahan tum aur hum
nahi rahe guzar gaye.
Aaj bhi yaad hai wo,
chandini raat,
aur raat me woh
gum sum se baat.
Na jane kahan chala
gaya jese,
dhundne me bhi wese
din ab kahan milte hai.
Tumhare bina to ye,
chandni raat bhi,
adhura lagta hai.
Shayad tumhe yaad nahi,
hum inn chandni raaton
mein apne bhavisya ki,
baate kiya karte the.
Pata nahi ye sab kab,
poora hoga.

–Abhilash Rout
(IG: @coolcapt_abhilash)

Chand _Open Letter

My dear chand,
You are so frigid whatever happened around you, you won't change your originality for other's sake this is the one which captivates me towards you because I never glimpse this tremendous manner in this physical world where I used to dwell. No one can understand the subtle relationship between you & me. whenever I felt like a hell by residing here without any delay I just make haste to the terrace to see you, my love but you culprit play a hide and seek, at that time you just conceal yourself by the midst of the cloud. I felt like hades but you can't even see myself sad within a minute with your bright smile, you just come in front of me and agree with your downfall.in that meantime I just forget all of my concerns, grieves, stressful impressions and all. You are a great mentor to me because you only taught me the truth of existence, the darkness is a small thing in front of our Brightest upcoming. my dear angel how could I equalize all your abundant affection. Without you am none here thank you for exhibiting the actual me. "You are the one who made my hell_like heaven, you are the one who shows the luminous path even though in the dark hues, you are the one who taught me the compassion by your hearty glints, you are the one who tends me from the deepest valley of adversity by the lovable touch on my clumsy skin, you are the one who makes me feel precious by your abundance of love". Thank you is just a nano word for your unconditional love towards me chand, no more words are discovered till now to endorse about you. I wanna say a huge love you, to my love.

With ample of love,
Your dark angel......

~S. Aarthi

(IG: @theseekerquote)

Chand

Ek rooz yunhi baaton baaton main,
Unsae mili anginat soogaton main,
Hum ek cheez sae roobaru huvae,
Voh cheez dour thi buhat ,
Par kareeb si lagi voh buhat,
Voh chand tha asmaan ka
Jo angan main hamari har raat milta tha,
Voh apna toh na tha ,
Par kisi apnae sa tha,
Uski justajoo toh na thi,
Par usko kashish buhat thi,
Voh kehtae the har baar pehlu main beth k,
Ik rooz chaand ko dekhaen gae teri goaed main laet k,
Voh khawheshaen adhuri si lagti hai,
Us chand k saath honae sae puri si lagti hain..

- Meer Aarifa

(IG: @Meer_aarifa)

My Love And The Moon

Gazing deep into your eyes,

I see a gentle glow reflecting from above

While lying underneath this moonlit sky.

The silvery beams cast soft upon your skin,

As you lie so close to me arms and legs

Entwined in a lover's embrace

The pink gloss of your lips

Seems to glisten in the moonlight's gentle glow

Lips begging to feel the tender touch of mine

The moon's gentle beams softly beckon us to continue our song of love,

For you are the poetry that makes my heart sing

And I the melody of your words

And together the beating of our hearts compose

A poetic song of love.

May our symphony of love underneath the moonlit sky

Last a thousand lifetimes.

O moon, shower your everlasting glow and shine,

To make our love growing eternal and divine.

-Abhishek Rawat

Amidst The Sky

Rusted from the last night rain

I waited for the sun to rise,

Washed over in grass and muted blues until the sky finally caught

fire !

Light kissed the edges of clouds

Everything bathed in shades of amber.

Standing beside the window

I tried catching the skies with my eyes.

The splendid and endless world to touch.

The moon could be seen again flickering amid stardust.

The moon followed that path again, the known address to the never

ending space in between my contemplation and then,

Slowly the moonlight passed through caressing my soul and with

brushstrokes painted the canvas of the sky,

and I woke up again

With wings to fly.

−Disita Sikdar

(IG: @disitasikdar)

ऐ चांद तेरी रोशनी ने..

रात के अंधेरे में
सपनों में उज्यरा कर गया
ए चांद तेरी रोशनी नें
गज़ब का कारनामा कर दिया;

सुकून की चादर ओढ़े
शीतल छाया तले
सपनों में ऊर्जा भर गया
आए चांद तेरी रोशनी से
सपनों को किनारा मिल गया;

दिन के उज्यरे में
करते हैं सभी मेरे सपनों की निन्दा
पर आए चांद तेरी रोशनी से ही हैं
मेरे सपने ज़िंदा;

सपनों को खूसूरत हकीकत
का रंग मिल गया
आए चांद तेरी रोशनी से
मेरे सपनों का कमल खिल गया;

ज़िन्दगी में खूबसूरत हकीकत का पंख
सपनों से जुड़ गया
आए चांद तेरी रोशनी ने
सपनों को उड़ना सीखा दिया;

रात के अंधेरे में
ज़िन्दगी में हजारों रंग भर गया
आए चांद तेरी रोशनी ने
मुझे जीना सीखा दिया!

-Najudah Tabassum
(IG: @tabassumwajdah)

चांद सी मुस्कान

अक्सर चांद सी मुस्कान ओढ़े

बादल सी बलखाती कुछ यूं नज़र आजती हो ,

एक बार को तो चांद भी शर्मा जाए ,

कुछ यूं मुझे देख इतराती हो ,

दीदार को तुम्हारे तरस सा मैं में गया हूं ,

जिस तरह चांद की चांदनी सूरज की देन है ,

कुछ उसी तरह मेरी रगों में तुम बसी हो ,

अक्सर चांद सी मुस्कान ओढ़े

बादल सी बलखाती कुछ यूं नज़र आजती हो ,

ईद के चांद सा जब जब

तुम यूं छिप सी जाती हो ,

इस जान की जान हलक तक आकर

रुक सी जाती है

जो दीदार हो जाए तुम्हारा ,

पूर्णिमा की तरह मेरा चेहरा जो खिल जाता है

क्या नुमाईश करू मेरे माथे पर शिकन की

तुम अक्सर इन्हे अपनी एक

झलक दिखा कर मिटा देती हो ।

अक्सर चांद सी मुस्कान ओढ़े

बादल सी बलखाती कुछ यूं नज़र आ जाती हो

~Sachin Banoudhiya

(IG: @Sachin_banoudhiya)

!! ये चांद है या तू !!

दूर भी है, गुरूर भी है।

नज़रों के सामने भी है, और हर शाम सबके लबों पे तेरा नाम भी है।

तू है तो जैसे जगमगाता जहान, तू ना हो तो शमशान आसमां।

जगह जो तेरी है उसी से रात सुनहरी है,

तू दूर होकर भी मेरी नज़रों का पेहरी है।

!! शर्माता चांद !!

- क्या कहूँ तेरी इस अदा पे,

तू यूँ चुप रहकर भी , मुझसे गुफ्तगू कर लेता हैं।

- क्या लिखूं तेरी इस अदा पे,

के इतने सितारों के बीच भी तू , छिपने के लिए बदलो का सहारा

लेता हैं।

-Sumit Sharma

(IG: @_sumitt.sharma_)

Imprinted Regolith Love I Have

It was the silent world I've ever met,
It was the beautiful moments that embraced me,
It was the creepiest moments that shook me,
Why does this love possess a mysterious wandering?
To the heart's God you may ask a thousand questions,
Yet the heart will give a puzzled clue,
The amazement,you are looking upon ever after,
Keeps your life swirling through twists of fate.
You shall know it for your crystal bright mind,
There was always a shelter under the darkness,
The brightest darkness,comforted your smile.
The deepest darkness , challenged your fears.
For all your mortal life,shall be a crater,
A crater holding innocent anxieties,
A crater holding permanent survivals,
Where regolith imprints your proud life.

~Swetha D

(IG: @thedreamyworld07)

चांद और मेरा महबूब।

चांद को देखता हूं तो चैहरा उसका नजर आता है साथ में छोटा सा तारा अपने होने का एहसास दिलाता है

जब हमारी बात नहीं होती है तो मैं चांद से बातें कर लेता हूं और जब हमारी मुलाकात नहीं होती है तो मैं चांद से ही मुलाकात भी कर लेता हूं

चांदनी रात का भी एक खुबसूरत एहसास होता है और जनत तो तब मिलती है चांद की चांदनी में बैठ कर बातें करने से जब हमारा महबूब हमारे साथ होता है

चांद आशिकों का सहारा है जो अपने दिल की बात नहीं कह सकते, जो एक तरफा प्यार करते हैं वो चांद से बातें करके मुस्कुरा लेते हैं

अब और क्या लिखूं चांद के बारे में बस हर कोई चांद में अपने महबूब, अपने चाहने वाले को देखता है।

-Sourav Bhatia

(IG: @_souravbhatia_official)

स्वीकार

चलो कुछ सपनों को याद करें,

जो भूल गए हो तुम वह बातें स्वीकार करें।

सपनें टूटे हैं लाखो मगर,

उन सपनों को जोड़ एक नई शुरुआत स्वीकार करें।

होगें कई लोग तुझे भटकाने वाले,

क्यों ना सही रास्ते की तलाश कर उस मंजिल को स्वीकार करें।

माना कठिनाइयाँ आई हैं बहुत सी ज़िंदगी मे,

सपने तेरे आसान नहीं यह बात भी स्वीकार करें।

तू योद्धा हैं इस संघर्ष भरे युद्ध का,

चल युद्ध पूरा कर उस जीत को स्वीकार करें।

-Reena Karamdev Yadav

(IG: @Poem__gallary)

Woh Raat

Uss chand mein
Ek alag hi kashish thi
Uss raat ye nazar
Tumse jo ja mili thi
Labon pe hmare
Ek khamoshi si thi
Par inn ankhon mein
Madhoshi si thi
Ye dhadkan pas aane ko
Mano betaab si thi
Par ye dooriyan
Hmesha se barkaraar hi thi

~Poorvi Verma

(IG: @Poorvi98)

Moon and You

When I walk with the moon,
I feel you nearest just beside my heart.
When I look at the moon,
I see your face shining bright like numerous stars.
When I talk to the moon,
I hear your voice answering back to me.
When I sing to the moon,
I hear your melodious hymn buzzing around me.
When I dance with the moon,
I feel you holding me closer and kissing my forehead.
When I read adventurous stories to the moon,
I can visualize you, my Knight, my lover.
When I sleep on the lap of moon,
I feel you closest, humming a sweet lullaby and watching me
to sleep.

–Debanjana Ghatak

(IG: @dgwrites_)

(1)

"Tmne apne pyar ko chand keh diya,
Or chand n apne daago ko ,
tmhare samne rkh diya!
Vo toh kher insaan tha
Chand n kha lo m bhi bdl gya" !

—Kartik kumar

(IG: @tales_that_bleed_02)

अकेला चाँद

वो भी क्या दिन थे
चाँद को देखते-देखते ही सो जाते थे
जब माँ लोरी सुनाती थी

वो कभी गम नही मेहसूस करता
अकेला चाँद वो हमेशा खूश रहता है
चाँद सबको हँसाता है

वो हमें रात में सहारा देता है
गरजूओंको रोशनी भी देता है
चाँद भी हमपर बहुत सारे उपकार करता है

चाँद का रूप ही अलग है
जब भी हम देखते थे ऊसे
आज तो हम भी उसपे फिदा है

–Sangram Santosh Salgar

(IG: @sangramsalgarpatil144)

Inspiration from The Moon

Whenever I'm look at the moon. I am thinks about the beauty of the moon. Because everyone compares beautiful things with the moon, especially their love.

But the moon is not only the symbol of love, like if you think different then outcomes also different. We can motivate from the nature of the moon. The Moon has a tendency to being dark and again brighter in every 15 days, thus we can assume or apply this phenomenon as in our daily life that is "Every bad days (dark) have a good future (brighter) so we just have to wait till the time changes.

Another best example is that the moon doesn't even have own light, But still smile and shine.

-Bickey Mandal

(IG: @bickey_ki_ankahi_baatein)

My Dear Love

Who said I am alone while walking in the night;
My partner is there moving with me in the sky on my right;
Showering on me his sparkling light;
Which makes me much more delight;
With a blush on my face so bright:
Dear love, could you come from such a height;
I am waiting for your alight;
To convey you good night.

-Dr. Harini Chowdary Vadlamudi

(IG: @leeni_1406)

में और चांद

उस रात चांद की आंखो में नमि देखी ,

शायद उसने भी मेरी

तन्हाईयो का अंबार देखा ,

उसने भी शायद मेरे जैसे

अपने करीबियों को खोया होगा ,

शायद उसने भी अपने ,

हर लम्हे में सदी खोई होगी ,

उसने भी मेरे जैसे

गमों का मौसम देखा होगा

तभी तो वो भी आधा सा

निकलने लगा है ,

आसमां में कभी कभी ,

जैसे हम निकल पड़ते है

कभी टूटे से तो

कभी बिखरे बिखरे से अपने घर से ,

चांद भी रोया होगा ,

मेरे गमों को देखकर

मेरे साथ सुबह की

पहली किरण निकलने तक ,

आखिर इश्क़ भी एक अमृत है

जब तक वो ज़हर ना हो जाए ,

क्योंकि अगर इश्क़ ज़हर हो गया तो ,

इश्क़ अपनी पहचान खो देता है

चांद ने भी छोड़ा होगा बहुत से

तारो को अपनी राह में ,

जैसे हमने भी छोड़ा है

कितनो को अपनी राह में ,

चांद ने भी अपने आप

को बुझाकर बैठा लिया है ,

इन सितारों की महफ़िल में

जैसे हमने बुझा लिया है

इन चमचाती दुनिया में ,

रुसवाई तो चांद को भी मिली

सितारों के आगन में

रुसवाई हमे भी मिली

मोहब्त के फैले आनगन में

मगर चांद को भी हमने

हमारी तरह शायराना होते देखा है

-Shivansh Sharma

(IG: @Shivanshrockzzzzz)

56

Chaand Apne Mohabbat Ka Gawa Hai

Naa jane kab wo raat hogi,
Jab zuba pe mohabatt ki baat hogi,
Tadap rahi hai yeh aakhe tumhe dekhne ko,
Ruk rahi hai saase tumhe mehsus kerne ko,
Na jane kab wo raat hogi,
Tere aur mere mohabatt ki izhar hogi..

~Paulami Kotal

(IG: @_khwabon_ke_parindey_)

A Full Moon

Moon seed, nestled in rich belly soil
Seeking a place in which to uncoil
Fertile thoughts gone now, allow you to flow
Wise woman's wisdom with your stream does grow

Moon seed, sweet source of maiden fruit
Shine upon me, so my soul will take root
Illume my dreams, sweep shadows aside
Come, christen me in your crimson tide

Moon seed, your blessings so full
Drip slivers of wisdom in my heart pool
Lift spirit veils on my dry river bed
Come, let your tendrils across me spread

Knowing my harvest will soon be past
I cling to your tears as if they're my last
Moon seed, flow top my rivers deep
And take hold, so your light I may reap

-Chahat Batra

(IG: @_chahatbatra_)

The Loveable Moon

A loveble moon; you shall always be a diamond the cosmos that I see like the snow that glitter white like your faith that shines bright you bring out the best in me.

When I stand before the sky blue and with white stars I feel a gentle embrace intended just for you.

When you see a pearl or shell in the eyes of mine, know it is me talking you by the hand know your heart and soul.

Will renew a grand and epic love for you or a single hearted love for you.

From my heart to the back and front of you, I loved you a lot...

Whenever I look up at the starless sky alongwith you then who should be there sharing the loveable moment with me, this moment that hold has no significance for my life.
The source of strength from a long distance with words that I have none to give with hope and love, may your shine live like more than a shining star

While I look your absence at up, I miss you the most dear...

-Yash Ojha

(IG: @im_rockstar_03)

चांद सब जानता है

चांद की सरगोशियां बड़ी ही सुहानी होती है

क्योंकि चांद तो सब देखता है और सब जानता है

चांद हर सच्ची कहानी का चश्मदीद गवाह होता है

जिसे वह अपनी रोशनी से बयां करता है

कौन सच्चा है और कौन झूठा चांद ये बखूबी जानता है

कहते हैं इस धरती पर कोई अकेला नहीं आया

उसका जोड़ा भी कहीं ना कहीं इस धरती पर साथ आता है

और चांद हर जोड़े को बखूबी पहचानता है

चांद से हर प्यार करने वाले प्यार करते हैं

क्योंकि चांद ही तो है

जो हर प्यार करने वालों को जोड़ता है

इसलिए तो चांद की सरगोशियां बड़ी ही सुहानी

और बड़ी ही प्यारी होती है

~Saloni Lal Srivastava

(IG: @salonilalsrivastava)

चाँद गवाह है

कभी मील वो अकेले में,
तो बैठकर उसे सुनाऊँगी।
प्यार में क्या वजह क्या बेवजह है,
मेरी मोहब्बत का वो चाँद गवाह है।

आधी रात को जब मैं रोई थी,
इस दिन मैंने अपनी चाहत खोई थी।
कहता कोई मग़रूर तो कोई बेपरवाह है,
मेरी मोहब्बत का वो चाँद गवाह है।

लबों पे हसी का उजाला था,
दिल में दर्द का अँधेरा था।
मैंने उसकी कदर नहीं कि ये अफवाह हैं
मेरी मोहब्बत का वो चाँद गवाह है।

मैं मरती थी सौ मौतें उसके दुःख पे,
उसकी खुशी के लिए मेरी आँखें तक भरती थीं।
कहीं ज़िंदा हूँ मैं या अब मेरा घटवाह है,
मेरी मोहब्बत का वो चाँद गवाह है।

-Grishma Ninave

(IG: @grish_ninave)

हाय चंदा

तेरी मेरी साथ की एक छोटी सी स्टोरी

तेरा यूं चांदनी रात में याद आना

और यू याद आकर मुझे तड़पाना

यू तेरा हल्के से मुस्कुराना कर सताना

मुझे याद है तेरा,

मेरा अफसाना है बड़ा पुराना

यू चांद में तेरा नजराना

हाय ये तेरा कातिलाना

अंदाज है बड़ा पुराना

यू चांद को देख कर

तुम यूं उसकी तारीफ करती

और मुझे लगता कि

उस चांद की औकात ही नहीं

तुम्हारे सामने ,तुम्हारा नूर ही

किसी चांदनी रात से कम नहीं

तुम्हें याद है वह चांद का बादलों में छुप ना

अक्सर मुझे ,तुम्हारा सफेद दुपट्टे में

अपने चेहरे को छुपाने जैसा लगता है

तेरा दूर जाना अमावस की काली रात जैसा लगता है आज तेरा

फिर से यूं मिलना, बातें करना

वह हसीन चांद

को निहारने जैसा लगता है

-Arju Tiwari

(IG: @arju.tiwari.182)

चाँद सा चेहरा

निगाहों में बशा एक चेहरा था,

मेरे ख्वाबों में उसका पहरा था,

जब जब याद करता था उसे,

तब तब यादों में वह ठहरा था,

चांदनी सी उसकी मुस्कान है,

कुछ भी कहो वह हमारी जान है,

हरकतों से थोड़ी नादान है,

फिर भी यह दिल उसपे कुर्बान है,

मोहब्बत का यह अनमोल सा बंधन है,

लगता है जैसे दो दिलों का यह संगम है,

गुस्सा करूँ तो मनाने भी आए,

मान गया तो फिर से नखरे दिखाए,

उसके साथ रहूँ तो वह बहुत सताए,

किसी और के साथ देख वह जलती जाए।

—Abhiraj Gautam

(IG: @rising_pen)

(1)

Lying on the terrace, I saw the daughter of the cold shining moon in the quiet wide sky.
The mind was at peace ...
 In thought My mouth smiled at the magazines without me knowing ...
 Were those cloud masses jealous of it?! ..
Disappeared from me ...
My smile also disappeared ...

Today my eyes watered forever ...
Did the wind make me cry?! ...
The moon pulled the clouds away from the daughter ...

 After leaving the cloud, I saw there,
 The daughter of the moon looked at me as if she was lying, throwing a light of sincere laughter and asking, "Why are you crying?"

I wiped away the tears,
Without knowing the cause of the tears ...
Again peace of mind settled in the mind ...
Which thought is unified ...
I am still love with her..

~S Prakash

(IG: @s_prakash_prince)

ज़िन्दगी में एक रात ऐसी भी आए

चांदनी से आबाद काला - नीला आसमां हो

चांद को घेरे टिमटिमाते तारे हो

और तेरी बाहों में सिमटा हुआ मैं।

डूब जाऊं जिनमें, वो नशीली आंखें हों

खो जाऊं जिनमें, अदा में तेरी वो मस्तियां हों

और तेरी बाहों में सिमटा हुआ मैं।

सुबह तक ना ख़त्म होने वाली बातें आंखों से हों

उन्हें सताने के लिए की गईं शरारतें मनमोहक हों

और तेरी बाहों में सिमटा हुआ मैं।

तेरी रूह का जाम मेरा जिस्म चख रहा हो

तेरे जिस्म की खुशबू मेरी रूह में उतर रही हो

और तेरी बाहों में सिमटा हुआ मैं।

यही तमन्ना रब से हो,

खुदा की इतनी सी रहमत हो

ज़िन्दगी में एक रात ऐसी भी हो।

- Megha Arora

(IG: @_._._megha_._._)

Sea, Moon And The Shackles Of Earth.

Sea and moon are lovers of old times,
Millions of miles apart, but together they chime.

Sea is vast yet still and calm,
The moon is far yet ready to drown.

He revolves around the earth in pursuit of his love,
His obsession for sea too desperate to be curbed.

Sea too loves the moon but is imprisoned by the shackles of
earth,
He constantly rise to finally break free but fell back again like
a wingless bird.

Both sea and moon are well aware of their fate,
They are allowed to love but not enough to embrace.

But still the moon keeps revolving and the sea constantly rise,
They are waiting for the moment when their worlds will finally
collide.

When galaxies will burst and no one will remain alive,
Amidst the chaos two old lovers will finally unite.

Moon is a man and so is the sea,
Their love for each other is immense,
The shackles of society is what they are trying to break free.

~Karan singh

(IG: @Iamkaran08)

Moon, My Beloved-

Moon is the reflection of PERFECTION,
which is complete with its flaws.
Which hide in the ray of Sun,
Moon is the witness of those emotions.
Moon is calm just like my beloved,
it gives me peace, reminds me his love.
It's the secret keeper of my heart which holds all my
emotions,
it's shine washes away my stress, like the smile of his face.
The black spots moon, make it normal
like the anger, of my beloved.
Excess of goodness too can be harmful
like how excess truth of Yudhishthir did.
The sky become restless when
the moon hides from night.
Oh! My beloved, never do this to me,
I don't have the patience of sky

-Ishani Durba Purkayastha

(IG: @ishanidurba)

<u>सब हां, सब जी हजूरी है!</u>

हमारी मोहब्बत भी तो कुछ ऐसी है,बिल्कुल चांद जैसी है,
अंधेरों में उजाला है,रोशनी है वहां, जहां काला है ||

मुश्किलें भी सब आसान है, दिल में छुपा जो तुम्हारा नाम है,
वाकिफ है तेरी कातिल नज़रों से भी,छुरियां चलाना, तुम्हारा पुराना
काम है ||

पर ना जाने अब हम कुछ खोए से लगते हैं,रातों को जाग कर सुबह
सोए से लगते हैं,
हां, यह है कशिश तेरी, तेरा ही मुझमें नूर है,कुछ है तुम्हारा, कुछ यह
चांदनी रातों का कसूर है ||

सुना है,महबूब और हसीन कातिल हो जाता है,चांद का लिबास जब
जिस्म पर पड़ जाता है,
फिर तो सब हां, सब जी हुजूरी है,इसलिए कुछ मुलाकातों के लिए
चांदनी रातें जरूरी है ||-

Payal Singhal

(IG: @psinscriptions)

चांद की मन्नत

चांद की नजरबंदी ना हुई,

मोहब्बत की जैसी रीत हो गयी...

देखो चांद आ गया,

अब पूरी ये मन्नत हुई...

-Pratiksha Ghatge

(IG: @Pratiksha_Ghatge)

(1)

Once I believed that his
presence made be believe
nights too can twinkle
as his reflection changed
darken nights to moonlight
and made my heart beat
more happy and tight.
Unfortunately, presence
fade up just like a night
that has light but no
moon that could shine and made my heart
work happy and tight once again for lifetime

-Abha Bindal

(IG: @unknown_facts1523)

Full Moon

When all stars escape and hide in moon;
When the brightness condenses in milky whiteness;
When the water and earth glisten with silverness;
When the moon seems to quiver in sky's spoon.

When it becomes the glowing eyeball of the pond's eye,
The silent deep pond embraces it in its watery arms.
Meadow-men lay on the harvested hays in the farms,
Only to let their hardened bodies to be softened with sigh.

Somewhere, a lunatic bird coos in a woods yonder;
My self merged with the bird that is staring at.
My fancy is tantamount to the bird wants to reach that.
It is the full moon that always dwells in wonder.

-Vickey David

(IG: @vickey_david2)

Forever Amorous

Intertwined we stood beneath the radiance of the moon,
Clinged to warm ourselves ;
Feeling each other's heart throb-
 the transcendental exchange of aura
I could feel his breath on my shoulders .
Reticent though I was --
I clasped his broad chest – our lips reluctantly interlocked,
The taste of his saliva entered my mouth.
Our bodies immersed into the elixir of love,
engulfed by the effulgence of the moon-
Which stood smitten by our passion
Witnessing the gush of emotions :
Betwixt two intensely obsessed lovers -
enkindled by the incandescent moonlight .

– Manali Chowdhury

Meri chandani

Vo din tha sayana
Vo rath thi sayani
dikhi muje thi vo pehli baar
 Aur dekhe Dil dhadkne laga baar baar.....

Vo chandani raath ti
Vo sabse pyari thi
usko deke aisa lagta tha ki Chand khud neeche uthar Aya ho
Aur sabko kushiya vaat Raha ho

Vo itni pyari thi ki
Chand bi usee sharmaya jata tha
jab mein uski tarif Chand se krtha tha
Tab Chand itna jaltha tha ki vo suraj ho jatha tha

Rone De Aaj Hamko Do Aankhen Sujaane De
Baahon Mein Lene De Aur Khud Ko Bheeg Jaane De
Adhoori Saans Thi, Dhadkan Adhoori Thi Adhooren Hum
Magar Ab Chaand Poora Hain Falak Pe Aur Ab Pooren Hain
Hum

–Vikesh Krishna Jalmi Alias Gawde

(IG: @s_h_y__b_o_i)

Moon and Her

Whole day She use to keep quite,
She use to talk alot at night
Parents thought she was mad
But inside she was dead
Looking at the sky
She use to cry
No one can understand her pain
Looking at the moon she complain
She was just a way too down to earth
Are living for humans is that worth?
Moon was to high
But she could listen wind amplify
Easing her soul little bit
Telling her not to quit
Shown her each sight (phases)
Taught her the biggest lesson of life
No matter half or full just be always bright.
Moon accompanied her for rest of the life
Just a way better than any human bribe...

–Rakhi Krishnani

(IG: @Inkandfables_2607)

काश!!

काश...तुम उस सामने वाली गली में रहते...

थोड़ा दूर सही...मगर पास में तो रहते....

बिल्कुल उस चाँद की तरह...

आते-जाते यूँही मिल जाया करते ....

हर रोज़ मैं तुम्हें नए कुर्ते...नए झुमके पहन के दिखाया करती...

हाँ...पता है मुझे ...हमारा इश्क़ दूर है इन सब से...

मगर मैं सब कुछ करके...तुझे खुद में उलझाया करती...

रातों को अक्सर छत पर बैठ कर...तुझे और चांद को एक साथ निहारा करती....

बारिश के मौसम में ...यूँही तेरे सामने भीग जाया करती...

जो तू न आ सके मिलने कभी...मैं खुद ही आ जाया करती...

हर रोज़ कुछ नया बनाया करती...

हर रोज़ तुझमे खोने को...

ये जिंदगी बिताया करती....

काश!!

–Anita Zalwal

(IG: @शब-ए-वस्ल)

चाँद

अकेली रहने लगी हूँ,

ना कोई साथी, ना सहारा है।

बदलते हैं यहाँ दिन, तारीख, साल, रिश्ते;

पर एक चाँद जो नहीं बदलता, वो प्यारा है।

चाँद और आसमान का साथ सदियों पुराना है,

मैंने चाँद को अपना हमदर्द बना लिया ।

रोज खुली हवा में सोने के बहाने,

छत पर जाकर अपने दिल का हाल सुनाती हूँ।

लोगों को लगता है मेरा कोई मेहबूब है, जिससे में मिलने जाती हूँ;

मैंने चाँद को अपने सुख- दुख का साथी बना लिया।

चुपचाप वो मेरी बाते सुनता है,

लोगों की तरह नहीं, यहाँ की बात वहाँ करता है।

मेरे अंधेरे दिल को रात में भी रोशनी से भर देता है,

जब उसे देखती हूँ ,तो मेरी आँखों में अपनी चाँदनी की चाँदी भर

देता है।

-Parul Sunder

I Want To Love U Just Like Moon

I want to be with you just like,
the moon be with the sky.....
May be the way of making love keeps changing just like,
moon keeps changes it's shape....
But it will be last longer& keep growing
I want you to hide me behind ur back in disaster just like,
sky hides the moon during rain.....
I want to fill ur lyf full of happiness &
success just like,
sky gives light to the dark night....
I want us to be two perception with one soul just like,
the moon existence matters but it doesn't dominate the sky
colour.....
Just like moon I want us to shine#

-Tathambika

(IG: @Tathu895 (crazy thoughts)

Woh Chandani Raat

Badi hi haseen woh chandani raat thi
Jab humari pehli mulakat thi
January ka mahina tha
Chand lag raha sunhera tha
Mujhe aaj bhi yaad hai
Tune uss din peela suit pehna tha
Tu khidki pe aayi thi aur,
Mai chaaje pe khada tha
Halka sa phir tera sharmana hua
Teri iss aada ka chand bhi deewana hua
Phir toh milna humara aam hogaya
Charcha ishq ka humare sare-aam hogaya
Chand bhi gawah tha aur chandani nishani thi
Main tujhpe marta tha
Aur tu meri deewani thi
Bas itni si teri meri kahani thi
Woh chandani raat aur woh mulakat
Badi hi pyari thi

- Mausam.agrawal

(Ig: @mausam.agrawal)

Aey Chand Teri Alag Pehchan.

Aey Chand Teri Alag Pehchan hai.
Aey Chand tu kitno ka armaan hai.
Tu premiyon ki premika,
Tu kaie kaviyo ki kavita hain.
Aey Chand tu andhero mein roshni hain,
Tera roop jaise chashni hain.
Teri jhalak se mann ko milti hain khushi,
Aey Chand tujh mein dikhti hain muje muskaan aisi.
Tujhe dekhu toh mile ek sukoon,
Tuj tak pohochne ka hai ek junoon.
Aey Chand tujhe chhuna aasan nahi,
Fir bhi teri aor mann daudta hai.
Tere isharo pe suraj bhi rukh modta hai...
Aey Chand tujhe aisi kaie aur baatein bhi batani hai,
Tujhpar likhi maine bhi kaie kahani hai.
Naa jaane tu kitne sitaro ki jaan hai,
Mere sang bhi toh teri ek dastan hai.
Aey Chand Teri Alag Pehchan hai....

-*Priya Jogadia*
(IG: @priyapens)

मिल रही है चाँदनी उसके चाँदसे।

चाँद की चाँदनी में मानो जैसे प्रण लिया था प्यार नहीं करेंगे कभी

लेकिन देखो इस किस्मत ने कहा ला के रख दिया अभी,

प्यार भी हो गया है और इकरार भी

साक्षी थे बस चाँद चाँदनी तभी,

झगड़े भी होते है जैसे बीच बदल और चाँद की रोशनी

पर एक दूसरे बिना अधूरे लगते है जैसे चाँद के बिना चाँदनी,

कसमे भी खायी है कभी साथ न छोड़ने की

एक-दुसरे के अलावा इसी चाँद के नीचे जीने की,

मुलाकात जल्द हो यही है आरजू हमारी

पर क्या करें बहुत बुरी तरह से फैली हैं ये कोरोना की बिमारी,

सिर्फ देखा है चाँद ने तड़पना हमारा

किसको डर है क्या कहेगा जमाना,

जल्द ही मिलेंगे वादा है ये मेरा तुमसे

जैसे मिल रही है चाँदनी उसके चाँदसे।

– Vrunda Kumbhar

(IG: @vrundabharati)

(1)

सितारों की नुमाइश -

सितारों की नुमाइश में खलल पडता है,

चांद पागल है, अंधेरे में ही निकल पड़ता है,

अब सितारों की भी क्या बात करे,

वे तो आपस में ही लड़े झगड़े ऐठे हैं,

की जिस चांद को पागल बोले बैठे है,

उसी चांद के पीछे पागल हुए रहते हैं,

वो तो शुक्र मनाइए उस चांदनी की,

जो चांद को बचाए रहती है,

नहीं तो आज भी सितारे,

उस पागल चांद के पीछे ही घात लगाए बैठे हैं।

-Pragya Kapil

(IG: @hidden.vibes1011)

Moonlight Love

You, Your touch is like the day light,
It's like the sweetest pain,
That goldens my skin. Like a burning flame.
As your fingers run down my spine,
With my lips sweet red like the glass of wine,
As you sweep me away in your arms,
And the daylight fades away,
As I fall in love over again, with you.
Your love, Its like the moonlight,
Like the star in the moonlit sky,
Like a cresence that brightens the night.
Caresses the heart of twilight.
Brightens my day, sparkles my night,
As the darkness leads into the light,
In the beautiful abyss of the moonlight,
Under those skies as your arms hold me tight,
As I fall in love over again with you. Rises.
The euphoria is the nostalgia that, Incenses my skies,
As I let your love arise, Arise.
As I fall in love over again with you. With you...

-Mihika Saraf

(IG: @_mihikaaaaaaaaaa_)

Dazzling Beauty

Look !! Look !!
who is peeking through
the window screen ,
without my attention .
Ah !! What a pleasures sight ,
Its brightness blinds my eyes .
I gaze at the moonlit night at a glance ,
It seems ,
like a beautiful maiden has adorned nature , in a different
dimension.
I am sitting on a chair ,on the roof of my house enjoying the
pressure of tea in my hand .
The open sky all around ,
the gentle breeze and the moonlight seemed to change my
life .
For the first time in my life,
my poetic senses are awakened .
As much as
I got the realization of the beauty of the silver night I portray
in the language of my heart .
The rest is in the heart of the heart .

–Arijit Mondal
(IG: @arijitquotes)

चमक

चमक कर वो चले सितारो जैसे

दिल में एक उडान ले कर के ।

बादल में जैसे किसी चांद की उम्मीद लेकर के ।

प्यार भरी ऊंचाईयों कि चाहत लेकर के ।

चमक कर वो चले सितारो जैसे दिल में एक उडान लेकर के ।

~Stuti Mahesh Naik

(IG: @Stuti_nyk_02)

चाँद :- अनेकों पहचान

बचपन में मामा कहलाता ,
वक़्त के साथ चंद्रमा बन जाता ,

बच्चे मुझमे कहानियाँ ढूंढते ,
तो युवा अपने प्रेमी ,

कोई मुझमें अपने ख़ास
को याद करता ,
तो कोई अपने फौजी
की फ़रियाद करता ,

कोई मुझसे अपने दुःख बांटता ,
कोई अपनी यादों को दिखाता ,
कभी करवाचौथ पर ढूंढा जाता ,
या तो ईद पर याद पर किया जाता ,

ऐसे ही चल रहा है अपना
मान ,
दुनिया में चल रही अनेको
नाम से पहचान ।।

-Abhilash Sharma
(IG: @_ankahe_alfaaz__)

(1)

चाँद   अंधेरी रात की बात है चाँद से गले लगकर , किससे सुनाए है उससे , कभी दोस्त समझकर , कभी साथी समझकर , तो कभी मामा बोलकर । वो चमकता है रात को , छिप जाता है धूप में , मानो ज़िंदगी की असलियत है यह , रोशनी हो तो छिप जाए , अंधेरा हो तो रोशनी की किरण दिखाए । बचपन में पूछा करती थी मैं अपनी माँ से, बचपन में पूछा करती थी मैं अपनी माँ से क्या होता है चाँद ? तब सुना था मैंने , साथी है यह हमारा , रात को जहाँ चलोगे यह साथ दिखेगा । दोस्तो , अंधेरा है तो उजाला ले आओ अपनी ज़िंदगी में , साथ देगा चाँद , हर ख़ुशी में , हर ग़म में भी ।

–Diya Mehta
(IG: @diyamehta878)

चाँद से गुप्त गू

एक दफा फिर उस चाँद से कुछ बातें करनी है।

तो उनकी जो नजरें हैं ना, वो शांत समुद्र है।

जिसमें बस, डूब जाने का जी करता है।

और वो कहता है..

तुम्हारे माथे की बिंदी,

मुझे काली रात में निकले चाँद की याद दिलाती है।

और ये गालो की लाली है ना,

वो उसी रात में निकले तारों की तरह शर्माती हैं।

मेरे खुले केश हवा में यू तितलियों की तरह उड़ रहे हैं।

ए चाँद एक बात बताओ ...

तुम्हें किस बात का गुरुर है मुझे बताओ,

किस बात का घमंड कर यू आसमां में चढ़ चुके हो।

लगता है किसी ने तुम्हें आयना नहीं दिखाया,

लगता है किसी ने तुम्हें मेरे उन से नहीं मिलाया।

तो चाँद तुम जानते हो?

उनके होठों पर हसी देख हर गुलाब खिल जाता हैं,

उनकी आँखों की नमी से हर लम्हा मुझसे रूठ जाता हैं।

तो तुम्हें कुछ खबर भी है?

मेरे खुले केश जब उनके गालो को स्पर्श करते है,

दिन, दुपहर, शाम, रात हर तरफ बस उजाला करते हैं।

अरे तुम्हें कुछ पता भी हैं?

ना जाने किस बात का घमंड कर,

यू आसमां में चढ़ चुके हो।

घमंड करना बंद कर दो,

मेरा चाँद आ चुका हैं।

-Rani Singh

(IG: @_r_a_n_i__)

Shaam Hasin Ho

Chandni raat ho aur tera didar ho ,
Chand ki mitthi si chhaon mein tere sath guftagu ho .....
Bas itni si armaan hai dil mein tere sath har shaam hasin ho ,
Humari mohabbat ka bas ek chand gawah ho .....

Woh Aur Chand

Chandni raaton mein unse mulaqat hoti hai ,
Woh na nazar aayen to chand bhi rootha rootha sa lagta hai
.....
Aisa lagta hai jaise mere sath chand bhi intezar mein hai ,
Humare kaye sare yaadein aur waadon ka bas wahi ek gawah
hai .....
Unki pyari si hasi aur mithi si batein sun kar aisa lagta hai
jaise chand bhi muskura raha hai ,
Unki pyar bhari aankhe aur jhuki hue nazron ko dekh kar aisa
lagta hai jaise chand bhi sharma raha hai .....

~Parwana Bibi

O Moon

O thou moon white,
thou art shining so bright,
hast thou courage might,
fitting to answer my plight!
Thou art smiling wide
from behind the cloud,
gazing at my tears,
thou feel so proud?
Thy brightness would
remain no longer,
thou shalt not pass,
the fortnight this stronger!
Thou shalt be abated,
as the days would stroll!

1 Thou - You   2 Art - are   3 Hast - has   4 Thy - Your   5
Shalt – shall

−Isha

ऐ चांद

तू मुझसे जितना भी दूर हो पर बहुत पास लगता है,

तू उसके साथ होने का मुझको एहसास लगता है।

तुझसे यूं बातें करूं तो ये रात सुकून से कट जाती है,

तुझमें उसे महसूस करूं तो तुझमें मेरी दुनिया सिमट जाती है।

मगर फिर भी कई सवाल है मन में जिसके ज़िंदगी जवाब चाहती है,

क्या वो भी तुझे ऐसे ही देखता होगा,

जैसे मैं तुझे निहारती हूं?

क्या वो भी मुझसे मिलने की दुआ करता होगा,

जैसे मैं उसे पुकारती हूं?

ऐ चांद, बता ना,

क्या वो भी मुझे याद करता होगा,

जैसे मैं किया करती हूं?

क्या वो भी तुझसे मेरी बातें करता होगा,

जैसे मैं किया करती हूं?

क्या वो भी मेरे पास होने की हसरत रखता होगा,

जैसे मैं उस एक पल के लिए रोज़ इबादत करती हूं?

-ईशा

(IG: @pristinetales)

93

ऐ चांद - तेरा मज़हब क्या है?

ऐ चांद,

तेरा मज़हब क्या है?

तू हिन्दू का है और मुसलमान का भी,

कुछ करवा चौथ पर पूजें तुझे,

और कुछ ईद पर तेरी इबादत करते हैं।

तू दिन का है और रात का भी,

कुछ सवेरे से करें देखने की चाह तुझे,

और कुछ रात भर तुझे ही निहारते हैं।

तू मोहब्बत का है और जलन का भी,

कुछ देते अपने महबूब का दर्जा तुझे,

और कुछ तेरी खूबसूरती से जलते हैं।

ऐ चांद,

बोल तेरा मज़हब क्या है?

तू कहानियों का है और कविताओं का भी,

तू किस्सा किसी की पूरी ज़िंदगी का,

और तू हिस्सा किसी की नादानियों का भी।

तेरी चांदनी से होता ये जग रोशन,

तू अहम किस्सा कितनों की जवानियों का भी।

तेरा ज़िक्र ले आऐ नैनों में चमक,

और तू बना गवाह कितनों के अश्कों का भी।

ऐ चांद,

बता ना तेरा मज़हब क्या है?

~ईशा

(IG: @virtuous_soul17)

तुम चाँद हो उन गलियों की

तुम चाँद हो उन गलियों की

जहाँ कभी सुबह नही होती

जमा रहती है लोगो की भीड़ तुम्हारे घर के पास

वहाँ खड़े होने तक कि जगह नही होती

लोग निहारते रहते लोग तुम्हारे हुस्न को

जिनके देखने की कोई वजह नही होती

चाँद नाम से मशहूर हो तुम अपने शहर में

किसी और को चाँद कहने की हिम्मत नही होती

शुक्र है खुदा का हाथ थाम लिया है तूमने मेरा

वरना आज हमारी किस्मत में तुम लिखी नही होती

~ अभिषेक गुप्ता
(IG: @abhi_poetry)

O Moon

Moon Moon, shining bright
Looking us at the night
Do you love your beloved
Waiting for her till the night.

She too loves thou as you doth
Among the stars is she, your mistress
Too behold your beauty
As the city doth for whole the night.

Open upon the fields, you
Spread your beauty
It's your majesty to spreading lives
You are the symbol of mankind to the men

Men really love you for the selfless love
Thou art free to spread your shine
To the eternity of world,
As a best friend be always mine.

– Meenakshi Sharma

(IG: @meen.sharma12)

The Amazing Illuminator

The one that brings light into the dark night.
The one who sprinkles light on top of flower beds and trees.
The one who makes every single water glitter in rivers,
ponds, streams and valleys with it's own gorgeous gleeming
light.
Illuminator with it's bright white light playing pick-a-boo
with all of us each and every single night.
Effortlessly changing shapes.
Just to disappear all of a sudden one night.
When everything becomes dark and black.
And, stays like that till a small illumination of snow white
starts appearing the next night.
To be more precise it looks like a big snow ball.
I feel like going their to lie down and make snow angels.
To make small snow balls and through at friends.
To make a snowman there and when I come back to earth I
can see the snow man on top of the big illuminating snow
ball each night from my window.
The awesome Illuminator is our lovely Chand.
Our amazing moon!
Our amazing Illuminator!

-Dipti David

(1)

The love of moonlight is so beautiful that your heart melts trying to sink in the oceans of serenity.

-Chirag L Sagar

(IG: @chirag_cls18)

वादे

ए ग़ालिब खुदा मान बैठे उस चांद को भी,

इस तरह पागल था उसके इश्क में

चांद तो खुद छोड़ बैठे चांदनी को भी,

कहां वादे किया करते थे रात में

Corona Kaal

Yaad ayenge ye din
Ye subah der se uthna
Ye raat ko chand taankna
Yaad zaroor ayenge ye din
Ye roj roj ka kuch naya seekhna
Ye barso baad didi se milna
Yaad zaroor ayenge ye din
Ye shaam ko charcha karna
Ye saath me picture dekhna
Yaad zaroor ayenge ye din
Ye videocall par milna
Ye dosto ki galiyon ko bhi miss karna
Yaad zaroor ayenge ye MARCH ke din

-Ayushi bhatnagar
(IG: @Karavaan080)

Before The Coming Of The Night

Let the unsatisfied wish be fulfilled. Let my life feel happy joining feet in your steps. Let me be satisfied getting along with you.

Let me become your shadow not
leaving in any turn of the path. Many new beginning clearing the darkness.

Let the life missing out reaches its shore. your light of love brings a new essence of beginning. you are my love of everything.

Let the wait of long day show up my love and happiness. The moment where everything seems dark you shine like a diamond in the sky.

A pleasant shine poured in my smile
By telling it all filled in my heart today.

~S. Deeksha

(IG: @deekzz08)

Moon-My Nightcare Routine.

Ever since childhood moon gazing has been my nightcare routine. You probably would have seen hundreds of nightcare videos which would mention all the best creams, gels and balms. Acnes, scars, rashes need care and time to heal is so obvious to everyone but when it comes to inside it is not very obvious. The mental and social aspect of health are underrated until you have no choice but to check on.Letting go of the negative thoughts by analysing them and canceling them with the positives,is what I do,at the end of the day, I write my positive thoughts on the sky and the moon,the moon reflects light and shines,shines for me and my efforts and somedays where I don't have enough of me to introspect and make it, moon will still shine. Moon reflects light, it doesn't have light of its own, oh yes but Moon's legacy is not just it's light but it's depth and warmth in all it's shape.

Warm yellow light is just a add on, just like your night skincare routine is. But you aren't just about physical you are moonchild, you are more than scars.

Your beauty will outshine in darkness admist the scars, admist the light source.

–Disha Dulani

(IG: @dishadulani)

Waiting For You, My Silver Shine!

I am waiting for you to tell you something,
Things that I have kept inside my heart,
Thousand thoughts piercing in daylight,
One night with you my silver shine is all I want.

Now, when you've come tonight in the sky,
Shining brightly amidst twinkling stars,
I fail to keep my emotions within,
Give me a signal so I can begin.

A falling star signalled me to fill in,
That moment, a tear rolled down my chin,
Wiping it off, I began listing,
Countless harsh words of his that have hurt my soul within.

I know my love is pure,
Like your aura in the night light,
His love for me is fading seconds as they pass,
Should I let him go? Is what my heart asks?

~Richa Gupta

(IG: @im_richagupta)

Luna And Her Twilight

Cold nights and dusky moonlight, brings the remembrance of a person. The first time we met during the full moon, you were the sun which made me dance on dawn tune. Through the glass of the window, the lightning stroked. I witnessed the angelic face who grasped me with grace. Spark of fire was lit all over my body, the wind chimes started to wave agreeing that you are mine. You made my heart blossom with millions of flowers. But now you made me a new moon waiting for the lunar cycle with a lot of desire. The days spent with you were golden time. You drenched me in the rain of love and care. I am still the heartbroken Luna waiting for you my dear twilight.

– Vaishni Venkatesh

(IG: @vaishni_venkatesh)

The Orb Of Night

A ravishingly, fascinating comeliness she is,
Her felicity takes away all our solicitude,
She is a guardian Angel for the ones who lost their way,
For a lonesome heart, she is always there to soakup their sob ,
Admiring her elegance brings us peace of mind and stillness,
Sometimes she also clowned up like a letterdrop for the missing hearts,
She always soothe us by her serenity and reinvigorate our gash ,
Nevertheless, her surface is gloomy, she stood up lustrously,
I looked at her every night and blushed like a sunrise,
In the crunch, she will always be a covet box for all of us,
All-inclusive, she is a secret diary for a wallflower!!

~Shobhana serana

(IG: @sweety_shobz)

Mera Chaand

Andheri hai raat ,
Yeh andhera dilaye mujhe
 tere kami ka ehsaas,

Gumsum sa hai yeh samaah,
Dhunde tujhe yeh harr jagah,
Tere bin,
Murjhaya mera jahaan.

Baadlo meh se ,
koi zhake hai baar baar ,
Durr kre voh andhere ka ehsaas.

Chamchamaye voh apne taaro ke saath ,
Lo le aaya chaand apni chandni saath,
Fir jagmagaya mera jahaan ,
Durr hua gum ka tufaan .

Tere kami ko durr kre ,
yeh chaand taaro ka saath ,
Mere chaand tak pahuchaye mere dil ki pukaar ,
Hamare duriyo ko paas laye yeh chaandni raat .

-Aafreen Saleem

(IG: @Kuch_alfaaaz_aise_bhi)

(1)

Raat ke andhere mein,
Woh akeli laut rahi thi,
Uske dil mein ek daar tha,
Is andhere ki gehrai mein,
Ek khoaf tha,
Na kahi roshni hain,
Na kahi hain dil mein hausla,
Kya lagta hain andhere se daar??
Pucha is dil ne,
Dimag ne sunke thora sa socha,
Thora ghabraya,
Fir dhire se jawab diya,
Andhere mein rehta hain maan ka daar,
Yehi baatein sochte sochte andhere mein chal rahi thi,
Kuch ankhe jaise usko dekh rahi thi,
Koi peeche se usko bula rahi thi,
Par piche na murna hain,
Andhere mein firse na lautna hain,
Fir achanak se,
Jaise roshni ka barsat hua,
Andhere ka woh daar kahi kho geya,
Kaise hua yeh chamatkar,
Upar se aya yeh roshni ka bahar,
Andhere ko chirta hua suru hua hain yeh chand ka safar,
Zindagi bachaya hain firse us chand ne,
Andhere ke dhabbe ko saath leke,
Woh ab ek rakshak ban ke aya hain.

-Sayandeep Patra
(IG: @SammySamrat)

Chaand_

Ab tumse baat na hi sahi ,
Par yeh chand se rojana hoti hei
Sawal toh diloon mein kahi uthahte hein,
Par rozana chand se rubaroo
Kar bhi liya karte hein..

Ab pahele ki jese hamare bich
Baatoon ko le k faisley nhi hote,
Abhi toh sirf fasley hein
Aur yeh duriyaan jaan le jati hei..

Aj tum hamare saath na hi sahi
Par yahan aj v mehfil k jaan tum hi ho,
Abhi tumse baatein nhi hoti
Par roj tumhare bare mein baatein hua karti hein..

Ab toh hum v esh dil ko manna bethe
Ki yeh dil usse dil na laga jo bich choharaye chod gaya,
Dil ush chaand se laga
Kam se kam pyar ke naam pe bewafa na kahlayega

Yeh chaand aj tere daaman mei mera sar jhuka hei
Tere mohobbat ne hame sawara hei,
Yun kahein toh mujhe
Tumne zindagi jine ka ek naya jariya diya hei...

−Krushnapriya Behera

(IG: @pri_aashi_07)

Sharma Aati H

Aaj b yeh chandi raat gujar gaye tumari yaad ma ki
Aaj b yeh chandi raat gujar gaye tumari yaad ma
 ki thaak nhi gaye m aaj b tumara intazaar ma aaj b utni he
mohabbat h tumse jitni phela din se ti
Yaad aata h tumara har baat muja
Yeh chand sitara soona nhi data muja ab
Maan karta h aajo tumari baho ma
Pr shram se aati h is chand ki chandi se hume

-Dulgach pooja singh
(IG: @Sainamahi007)

When The Moon Sneaks ~

My memories of past,
set on a journey
in the local train,
which stops at every station,
to let those old forgotten passengers
to climb back in the coach,
and travel together to a distance.
At times the coach is full
and rest it is filled with known voices.
Slowly as we set on a return journey,
it starts emptying,
and till we reach the last destination,
the reality strikes back,
And I find myself
travelling all alone.
It was just a memory train,
in reality, people don't meet back,

when lost once...

~Ronak Jain (~ Janaab ...#)

(IG: @Ronak_rj_jain)

Love Letter

Dear Arudhima (Chipkali)

You know where I was last night? I was on the roof top of my house, watching the Sky, which seems so Beautiful, because of the billion and trillions of Stars, and A full Moon. Suddenly A thought crossed my Mind.
I went ahead with it, automatically.
I realised, The importance of You in My Life. I realised that You are The Moon of My Life.
Without Moon, We can't see Stars. Without You I can't see, The Beauty of This World.

The Stars will increase and decrease with The Moon, and one day both Moon and Stars vanished, and that day Sky was all alone with it's darkness, Restlessly waiting for that day, when Moon Came back with Stars in The Sky.

I was Scared, imagining that, you'll leave me one day. I can't put that feeling into words, it's Scary. After all these. I decided, this is the right time to confess My Love for You.

My life's empty like that dark Sky, and You're like a beautiful Moon and Stars and I wish for them to stay with me forever. Please fill My Life with your beautiful presence.

Waiting for your Answer
 Your Friend "Rudra" (Hippo)

-Jayant Jain

(IG: @Jayant9280_chhajed)

खूबसूरत-सा चेहरा

चाँद की चाँदनी में खूबसूरत-सा चेहरा देखा था। उस चेहरे को किसी से इतना प्यार हो गया कि उस चेहरे पर से चाँद जैसी चमकती मुस्कुराहट कहीं गुम हो गयी। चाँदनी रात का चाँद अमावस्या का चाँद बन गया मानो खिलते हुए चेहरे की मुस्कुराहट किसी ने छिन ली। इसी चाँद को साक्षी मानकर तुमने प्यार किया था। लेकिन आज वही चाँद बात करने में डगमगा रहा है। वही चाँद जो हमारे प्यार का प्रतिक था जो जानता था हम दोनो ने एक दुसरे से कितना प्यार किया था। हम इंसान अपने ख्वाहिशों में हमारे जिन्दगी में बहुत कुछ खो देते है और भूल जाते है कि आधा चाँद भी कितना खूबसूरत होता है।

हमारे प्यार का वह चाँद गवाह है। काले बादल जैसे उड़ते जुल्फें, बहती हवा और उसमें चाँद था गवाह लेकिन आज वह पल कहीं थम गये है। उस रात चाँद झूठा था। उस रात वह खूबसूरत-सा चेहरा किसी दुसरे का नही बल्की सिर्फ तुमारा था। चाँद भी खुद पर लगे काले दागों को भुलाकर पुरी रात चांदनी में खोता है और सुबह उससे बिछडता है। उसको अपने यादों में बसाकर। तुम भी बिलकुल चाँद की तरह ही हो। पास होकर भी पास नहीं। अगर तुमको दोबारा किसी से प्यार करना हो तो ऐसा प्यार करना जो दिखना नहीं चाहिए लेकिन प्यार की येहमीयत समझ में आनी चाहिए। प्यार शुरूआत में पूनम

की रात जैसा होता है। हमें बहुत हसाता है और फिर उसपर अमावस्या का ग्रहण लग जाता है। बहुत रुलाता है। तुम मुझे बताओ जो चाँद मेरे आंगन में आता है वही चाँद तुम्हारे आंगन में भी आता होगा, तो क्या तुम भी चाँद से मेरी ही तरह बातें करते हो? हमारे मिलने और बिछड़ने की यादों में।

-रेशमी महेश्वर वर्णेकर
(IG: @reshmi vernekar)

A Story Of a Beautiful Night

There was no moon; the stars just beginning to appear. A bend in the road, and a light shining from a hurricane lamp swinging outside a small roadside hut.

The clouds part and the moon appears - a full moon, bathing the mountains in the bright yellow light. Darjeeling basks in the yellow moonlight, each lighted dwelling a firefly in the night.

'Darjeeling - The Queen Of Hills' is always enticing. Suddenly the rain stops. The Clouds begin to break up , the morning sunshine strikes through the mesmerizing Kanchenjunga.

The view of the romanticizing moon will always stay in my heart forever. The shining moonlight of Darjeeling take me back to my childhood memories and ever since then I became a Selenophile person.

-Rittwika Sharma

(IG: @rittwika_sharma)

Moon-Minded

The beautiful face of yours, that clinges in my mind,
For you a melancholic night is also get brighten everytime!
 How can you be so kind?
Where the empty dark nights is no less than a sip of wine.

 How can something be so beautiful and still have no pride?
The authentic piece takes one to a beautiful memory ride!
Standing in silence, and gasping at you;
Number of questions arises with no clue.

Can someone love the stars more then the moon does?
But the love with no conditions and in no time the ages pass.
The reflection of yours on the water;
Creates a different scene of the night all together.
Even the bower glides in your presence;
And wonders about your beauty with a mixture of all the
essence.
As I lay and watch the sky,
You being the most beautiful always catches my eye!

You are the example of fondness;
Something which brightens the world in its darkness!
The epitome of authentic beauty!
The best story teller and an example of equity.

The strong dose of positivity;
Which shines bright , and spreads serenity.
There are no good byes to you ;
You makes the dark night bright, and thats makes you a
'perfect you'.

–Neha Chanda

मेरा चाँद

अब वो रातें वैसी हसीन नहीं

अब वो बातें वैसी दिलनशीं नहीं

जैसे पहले हुआ करती थी

पर हाँ, आज भी रात का चाँद बिलकुल वैसा ही है

जैसे पहले हुआ करता था

तुम ना सही मेरी बातें सुनने को

अब वो चाँद सुना करता है

वैसे मैंने तो पहले ही कहा था कि तुम चाँद से और मैं ज़मीं सी

इनका मेल मुमक़िन नहीं

पर तुम ना माने और तुम ख़ुद ही अलविदा कह गए

हाँ! सुकून है कि ये आसमानी चाँद बेशक़ मेरे पास है पर ग़म इस बात की

है कि, मैंने अपना चाँद शायद कहीं खो दिया !

—Jovita Ekka

(IG: @the_trouble_rhymer)

Moon

I've two sides of mine,
One is bright and happy,
The Other is dark and sad.
I sometime feel happy to the fulliest,
Sometime sadness engraves in me.
I change each day,
Sometime I'm half bright
And half dark.
I change accordingly,
I'm like humans.
Each day I can't be like a sun,
Sometimes I need to be like dark clouds.
Sorrows and happiness are part of me,
But, I'm beautiful and unique as thee.
I'm the moon,
With many imperfections
But, with a prefect existence.

–Megha P. Yadav

(IG: @megha_p_yadav)

Love Related To Moon Night

That moon night when we both met each other, can never be forgotten by me...

The way we held each others hands and walked on silent roads, can never be forgotten by me...

 The way he played with my curls and smiled, can never be forgotten by me...

Today also he is with me, Whenever I close my eyes and think about him he suddenly comes in my dreams and surprises me....

 I never met him in real but then also whenever he comes in my dreams I feel like...

That night will come; when we will be holding our hands and will walk on silent roads under the light of moon...

-Aarushi Singh
(IG: @_aarushi_21_)

Chandni Raat

जिसे देख हम जिंदगी जीते थे उसको देख जीने का तरीका भूल गए मरते रहे जिसकी यादों में याद किया तो आहे भरना भूल गए मुलाकात हुई थी चाँदनी रात में आखों से की बातें हम होंठ हिलाने भूल गए हर सांस में बसा हुआ था नाम उसका नाम लिया उसका तो हम सांस ही लेना भूल गए

~ Vikas Sharma
(IG: @9814vikas)

Eternal Love

Dark is miraculous as the shining moon in the dark looks fabulous.
Eternal love for moon does not let me live in Noon.
My shining eyes keeps on investigating the beautiful skies.
In search of moon,
 I spend my whole afternoon.
The existence of moon for me is the biggest boon.
Dear, moon I can see you, I can feel you and will always love you.

-Siya Golani
(IG: @ Siya_golani)

Chaand K Saath Chand Pal

Tanha andheri raat me,
Vo mera humsafar bana.

Mere aankho ki parat ko,
Usne apni roshni se chamka diya.

Safar tha mushkil,
Par usne mujhe ek lamha bhi akale naa choda.

Apne gol aakar se,
Usne meri drishtikone badal di.

Unn chand palo k darmiyaan,
Mujhe mohabbat hogai uss chaand se..

-Heena Shaikh Mulla
(IG:@theepoetryhub)

The Hunters Moon

The flame red moon, the hunters moon,
Looks along the hills, gently bouncing,
A vast balloon,
Till it takes off, and sinks upward
To lie on the bottom of the sky, like a gold doubloon,
The hunters moon has come,
Booming softly through heaven, lika a basoon,
And the earth replies all night,like a deep drum.

Do people can't sleep
So they go out where elms and oak trees keep
A kneeling vigil, in a religious hush.
The hunters moon hase come!

And all the moon lit cows and all the sheep
Stare upnat her petrified, while she swells.

Filling heaven, as if red hot, and sailing
Closer and closer like the end of the world.

Till the gold fields of stiff wheat
Cry "we're ripe, reap us!" And the rivwesy.
Sweat from the melting hills.

~Nilanjana Sarkar

Khwab Wo Adhoori Mohabbat Ka

Door hoke bhi wo paas hai
Khas uske hone ka ehsaas hai
Rutha hai jo mujhse bewajah hi
Uski narazgi se dil pareshan hai

Zidd unki hai dooriyan badhane ki
Aur zidd meri hai unhe manane ki
Asar chand ki chandni jaisa hai uska
Kaalii raaton ko intezar rehta hai jiska

Mere uss ishq ka wo gawah hai
Jo mera hai par use tera intezar hai
Mukammal na hua toh afsos toh hoga
Jo khwab adhoori mohabbat ke naam hai

Guzar jaati har raat usse niharne meh
Jise apna banana hai par mumkin nhi
Faslon ka soch ke darr toh lagta hai
Yeh ishq hai janab jo hadd kr deta hai

Uss chand se maine sifarish ki hai
apne iss chand ko manane ki
Jo meri zindagi ki chandni hai
Uske chehre pe muskan lane ki

-Jaspreet Kaur
(IG: @inkked_solace_)

ऐसा मुमकिन तो नहीं

इश्क़, मोहब्बत की बात हो
और चाँद का ज़िक्र ना हो,
ऐसा मुमकिन तो नहीं।
दो आशिक मीलों दूर हों
और चाँद उनके करीब होने का ज़रिया ना बने,
ऐसा मुमकिन तो नहीं।
एक नाराज़ हो किसी बात पर,
और दूसरा उसे चाँदनी रात में ना मनाए,
ऐसा मुमकिन तो नहीं।
चाँदनी रात में रोशन हो ये चाँद,
और महबूब को और करीब ना ले आए,
ऐसा मुमकिन तो नहीं।
ये चाँद जब-जब चाँदनी बरसाए,
तब मोहब्बत की बरसात न हो,
ऐसा मुमकिन तो नहीं।

—Astha Yadav

(IG: @ red_rose431)

Moony Love

A boy and a girl both resting under the open dark glorious night where the enormous sky is gloomed, beauteous moon splendors the entire globe and witnessing their sheer devotion for one another, shooting star falling over carrying infinite wishes multiplying the elegance of the universe and the pleasant silence rendering serenity to the souls. Gazing this beauty of nature, concurrently they shared a warmth together, beholding into each other's eyes, with hand in hand and kissing one another's forehead, they solemnly assured to love and promote each other aboundingly, lastingly, and wholeheartedly even after horizon vanishes evermore and the moon forgets to address night.

-Dr. Ruchita Chauhan

(IG: @the__real.thoughts)

ऐ चांद

दिखने में कभी अधूरे कभी पूरे हो तुम,
बादलों के पीछे छुप कभी मुस्कुराते हो तुम,
लेकिन ऐ चांद!
 सच में अपने में हमेशा पूरे हो तुम।।
किसी की अधूरी ख्वाहिश हो तुम,
आसमान में तारों के बीच भी अकेले हो तुम,
लेकिन ऐ चांद!
अकेले हो के भी खुश हो तुम।।
सबकी शिकायतें रहती है तुमसे,
नाराज़गी भी दिखाते है तुमसे,
लेकिन ऐ चांद!
सबकी चाहतों का पिटारा हो तुम।।

-Sandhya Kanojiya

(IG: @sandhyakanojiya19)

Oh My Dear Moon!!!

I wish I could see you over and over ;
Cause my obsession towards with you is never getting
lower..!
Your yellowish stain make me smile,
And your frost blue make me cry..!!
In the world full of galaxies,
I am just stuck with you ..!
May be because of your pitfalls ;
Or maybe because of your solitude..!
Sometimes I just sense that I'm just like you my dear
moon;
Cause I am dependent yet alone..!!
Having flaws yet still I bloom,
Want to show real face yet I can't fix upon..!
Oh my dear moon ;
Please just hold up there for sometime;
So that I can share,
My whole life ..!!
my whole rue with you..!!

–Divyanshi Goel

(IG: @ divz_goel)

Flairs & Glairs

Flairs and Glairs, a platform by a student for the students. We are esteemed youth struggling to carve out our path for our future and we follow a basic mindset Since everyone is not born with all-round skills. Joining hands with people who are born to execute it with perfection is the best way to evolve. Self-Evolution is the need of the hour but, evolving as a community is what we strive for. The initiative as kickstarted by, Founder-Mr. Shubham Shah with the motive to utilize the skillset and talent of writing has now a team of 10+ people who are actively participating into newer forms of learning and discovering talents among youngsters. We Provide platform and services like Publishing opportunities, Open mics, Workshops, Hands-on training. Operating with Brand Name Of Flairs and Glairs (Publication House), we offer the chance of elevating a passionate writer to an esteemed author With Brand name Teekhe Zasbaaat, We bring to you an opportunity to get accustomed with the Public Speaking and Presenting of Thoughts along with regular challenges to brush up your inking spirit. The newest initiative to extend our services we introduced in a new writing Platform- The Glittering Fables and Ink Over Tears.

We Choose to Fly Like A Falcon than to be a

Leg Pulling Crab.

To Know More: Infoline – 7781900870
Mail Us At-
flairsandglairs@gmail.com / info@flairsandglairs.in
Or Visit is at
www.flairsandglairs.com / www.flairsandglairs.in
Social Handles- @flairsandglairs @teekhezasbaaat

www.ingramcontent.com/pod-product-compliance
Lightning Source LLC
Chambersburg PA
CBHW070528160726
48003CB00004B/1733